THE MYSTERY OF THE
HAUNTED HOUSE

Ruby Yayra Goka

Sub Saharan Publishers

First published in Ghana, 2011 by
SUB-SAHARAN PUBLISHERS
P. O. BOX LG358
LEGON, ACCRA, GHANA
Email: saharanp@africaonline.com.gh

ISBN: 978-9988-647-87-2

Typesetting by Kwabena Agyepong
Cover design by Elkanah Kwadwo Mpesum

CHAPTER ONE

The Holidays Begin

Koku ran out of the classroom excited that the school term was finally over. He was both happy and sad. He was happy that there'd be no more school for six whole weeks. No more mental tests or quizzes or reading aloud or French conjugations for six whole weeks. No more waking up early and best of all no more homework!

He looked at his report card. He'd gotten 3 in English. That was worse than the term before when he'd gotten 2. He'd had 2 in Mathematics and French. It surprised him that he'd done better in French than in English. He'd gotten 1 in all the other subjects. His favourite subjects were Agriculture and Computer Science. He absolutely loved computer games and he loved to watch things grow. Last term, his Father had told him if he did not do better in English, Maths and Science, he'd get him a tutor to help him during the holidays and there'd be no more computer games for him. Koku knew enough to know that this was not a threat.

He could almost hear his father saying "How do you expect to get into a good secondary school when you can't even pass Maths and English." He sighed, then cheered up considerably when he looked at how happy everyone else was. He wasn't going to let his father's anger ruin his mood. He leapt into the air and did a little dance, enjoying the bright sun shining on his face. It was too good a day to waste on unpleasant thoughts.

He turned to look at his classroom; he waved at a couple of his friends and at his teacher. His school was quite big. It had classes all the way from kindergarten to junior high. The school was painted blue and white. Those were the school colours. Their uniforms were blue and white as well. The Ghana flag and a flag bearing the school's crest and motto 'Akoda bo nwa' fluttered in the gentle breeze. Though the motto of the school was a proverb in Twi, Koku liked it. Each term when they came to school, it was explained to them. In English, it's literal translation was "the child breaks the snail" but it meant that each child was to be recognized and given an opportunity. No limitations were to be placed on the child. The teachers wanted them to know they could be whatever they wanted to be.

Mr. Opoku the headmaster of the Junior High School section was trying to control the kids as they raced across the school compound. The short round man was having a hard time controlling the exuberant kids.

"Frema, make sure you practise your mathematics" he called out to a girl in Koku's class. She made a face but waved back happily and said; "I'll try, Mr. Opoku."

"No running," he called out to a group of boys who were running towards the football field but they didn't seem to hear him.

"Philip, tuck in your shirt." He yelled to another boy. The boy stuffed the front of his shirt into his shorts and continued on his way. Mr. Opoku wiped the sweat that was dripping down his face with his handkerchief. Though he would never admit it, he would miss the children terribly. Privately, he considered the school to be his nursery. It was up to him and his staff to provide the right environment for these children to grow and become useful and responsible citizens of the country. He considered it a scary task indeed that various parents had entrusted the care of their children to him and his staff. He took great pride in laying the foundation for these young fertile minds to attain their various potentials. He puffed out his chest. It was no mean task but he was proud to say since he put his hand to the plough nine years ago, he had never once looked back. The school had had a hundred percent pass ever since its students started sitting for the BECE (Basic Education Certificate Examination).

He looked around him with pride at the children as they said goodbye to their friends and teachers and prepared to go home. He would miss them all. He wondered what he would do for six whole weeks. He spied Koku under one of the trees. He knew Koku well; he was one of the boys who loved working in the school's vegetable garden. He called to him "Koku Amegatsey, come here."

The boy ran towards him. It was no use telling these children to walk. They run everywhere. Koku still had his report card in his hand. "How did you do this term?"

"Not too well," Koku said handing his report card to Mr. Opoku.

"You had aggregate 9 with 6 ones. That's good. You just have to do a little better in English and Mathematics."

Koku shook his head in disagreement. "My father won't think so. He'll say I should have had aggregate 6 with 10 ones like Sena."

Mr. Opoku remembered Sena well. She had been head girl the year before. She was currently in one of the leading senior high schools in the country. She had been one of the few to have aggregate 6 with 10 ones. She never had below 90% in the entire time she was in junior high school. She was a model student. It was not easy for Koku: his father expected him to fill his older sister's shoes.

"Ah, Sena... how is she doing?"

"She's fine. She's class prefect in her new school. We visited her in school last week, she will be on holidays in three weeks."

Mr. Opoku put a comforting hand on the young boy's shoulder. "Don't be so hard on yourself, young man. These are good grades, besides you still have two more years before you sit for the BECE, trust me..." and here he paused to stand straight. He straightened his tie, pulled up his trousers and puffed out his chest a little, and said; "by that time, you *will* be ready."

For Mr. Opoku's benefit Koku smiled. Mr. Opoku was talking about his *future* grades; his father would be disappointed with his *present* grades. The headmaster patted the boy's shoulder and walked away quickly to separate two boys who had started to fight. There was no way his father would be happy with these grades. Just no way. Mr. Amegatsey expected nothing but absolute excellence from each person in his household.

Koku's friend, Manuel, came running up to him. He was also clutching his report card and his 'our day' basket. He was all smiles. He had gotten 1's in all the subjects. Manuel was Koku's best friend. They would play football with the boys from the other form one class; then they would go to Manuel's house together till his father closed from work and came to pick him up. But first he had to check on Ami, his little sister.

"Come on, the other boys are waiting". Manuel said dropping his basket on the floor and putting his report card under it.

Koku hesitated a second. It was odd that Ami had not been waiting outside his classroom like she usually did. She was probably playing on the swings, he thought. He tucked his report card under Manuel's basket as well. He had not brought a basket of food. Manuel was the only boy in his class who had brought a food basket. Even some of the girls had not brought food and had asked their parents for money instead. The plan had been to save money to buy fried yam and turkey from Auntie Dee. She sold the crispest yam he had ever tasted. It was even better than what Mama fried at home.

Koku removed his shirt and hang it on the branches of one of the trees. He took off his sneakers and socks as well. Mama would not be happy if he went home all dirty, besides he loved playing football barefooted.

The boys quickly divided themselves into teams of eleven players each. Manuel kicked the ball and the game began. "Here, here!" Koku called to Akuffo when Akuffo got the ball and was looking for who to pass it to. Akuffo back passed to Koku who dribbled two defenders and shot the ball into the back of the net.

"G-O-A-L!" the boys roared, throwing themselves at him. He grinned. The boys lifted him high on their shoulders. He noticed Ami waving at him from the sidelines. He waved back. He was happy. He would miss playing football with his friends during the holidays.

CHAPTER TWO

The Strange Visitors

Naa Teiki was angry. Her mother had promised that Esi, their house help and the driver would take her to a fast food joint to buy fried rice and chicken. But Esi had woken up with a fever this morning. The driver had taken her to the hospital and they were not yet back. Mummy had promised to take her when baby Nene was asleep. But Nene had fussed and fussed all morning. Each time Mummy laid him down to sleep, he woke up screaming. Mummy said it was because his teeth were starting to grow.

Naa Teiki watched as he started howling again. She adored her baby brother. He could sit upright by himself and he could crawl. Most times she let him play with her but lately he had started eating her crayons so she hid them from him. He liked it when she tickled his tummy and said 'bah' in his face. That made him laugh then he'd stick his fingers into his mouth and smear saliva all over her face. Daddy called him 'the drooling machine.' But today 'the drooling machine' was 'the crying machine.' He squirmed and scrunched his eyes. His lower lip quivered then he opened his mouth revealing the pink ridges that were his gum. There was a minute of quiet then he started screaming. Naa Teiki stuck her fingers in her ears. She was tired of all the crying. How could one tiny baby make all this noise she wondered?

Mummy looked tired. Her eyes were red and she was yawning a lot. She strapped baby Nene to her back with her wrapper and started singing to him. His sobs grew quieter and quieter and finally he fell asleep. Then Mummy entered the bedroom. Naa expected baby to start crying again but she heard nothing. She waited for Mummy to come out of the room but Mummy didn't come.

She opened the bedroom door quietly and peeped in. Both Mummy and baby Nene were asleep on the bed. Naa Teiki didn't know what to do. Nene had been crying all night so Mummy hadn't gotten any sleep, neither had Nene himself for that matter. If she woke Mummy up and baby Nene also woke up who knew when he would go back to sleep? Besides, Mummy was tired; she didn't want to wake her up.

She looked at the 20 cedi note in her hand. Daddy had given her the money before leaving to work. She really wanted that fried rice and chicken and she couldn't wait till Mummy woke up. She wished the driver and Esi came back soon. They had been gone all morning. She had an idea. She would open the gate and wait outside for Esi and the driver. Naa Teiki was six years old. She was forbidden from going outside the gate by herself but surely just waiting outside wouldn't hurt, would it? Why hadn't she thought of it sooner? Yes, that's what she'd do. She'd go outside and wait for Sister Esi and the driver then they could go and get the food before Mummy woke up. She would even buy two. One for her and one for Mummy though she knew Mummy would not be happy if she found out that Naa Teiki had gone out of the house by herself. Her decision made she opened the gate and slipped outside.

She stood and stared down the road in the direction from which Sister Esi and the driver would come . The street was deserted. Naa didn't notice a taxi that was parked across the street from her house. She didn't notice that the occupants had taken a keen interest in her either.

After sometime, a woman stepped out of the taxi. She walked up to Naa. She was very pretty and had a dimple when she smiled. "Hello," the woman said. "You must be Naa Teiki, I'm your mother's friend, is your mother at home?"

"Yes, but she's asleep. Should I wake her up for you?"

"No, that's ok," the woman said quickly. She smiled again. Her dimple deepening. "I just want to leave something for her. It's in the taxi, come with me and I'll get it for you."

"Naa? Naa?" Mummy had woken up and was calling her.

Before Naa Teiki could answer, a man came out of the taxi and grabbed her. Mummy had come outside but she was too late. Both the man and the pretty woman rushed back to the waiting taxi which sped away. They had Naa Teiki with them.

Naa's 20 cedi note floated in the wind. Mummy began shouting for help but by the time the neighbours came out, all that was left of the taxi was a cloud of dust.

CHAPTER THREE

The Midnight Journey

"**L**et's go now," the man known as Jagger said as he came out of a hut in the middle of a forest. He wore a black shirt and black trousers and though it was night, he wore very dark sunglasses. A jagged scar run from the corner of his left eye to the commissure of his lip. The skin on his face looked burnt. "It's a very dark night; if we hurry we can make the journey in five hours instead of seven. The others will be waiting for us." "I have a bad feeling about this" the pretty woman he was talking to said, as she climbed into the passenger's side of the truck. Her name was Nancy. The trailer of the truck was filled with cows. "I think we are making a mistake in changing the original plan. Her parents are rich, what if....."

"That's exactly why we have to do this; once we get the money we can leave the country. We will never come back. Isn't that what you want?" Jagger checked to make sure that the door was secured at the back of the truck. He didn't want it opening and the cows falling out when he was on the road.

The woman sighed and looked up at the sky. It was very dark indeed. There was no moon and hardly any stars. The light that the few stars gave out was blocked out by the leaves of the huge trees in the forest. Few people knew this hut existed and even fewer still knew the road that led up to it. Even if the police had been tipped off, there was no way they could have followed them here. Jagger was never wrong, she trusted him but this time she could not shake off the feeling that something bad would happen. She sighed again. Jagger reached out and took her hand. "I promise this is the last time." He smiled at her but because of the ugly scar on his face he looked like he was in terrible pain.

She smiled and he started the truck. She settled back and tried to sleep but gave up. The road was full of potholes which the vehicle lurched in and out of.

At the back of the truck, Naa Teiki lay huddled in the corner. Dirty blankets had been used to cover her. The smell of the cows made her sick. She felt like vomiting. She hugged herself tighter and tried not to cry. The taxi driver had told her if she shouted or cried the cows would know she was there and they would bite her. Another man, the one with a scar that run from his left eye to the corner of his lip, the one called 'Jagger' had hit her the first time she cried. Jagger carried a sharp knife in his pocket. He had told her that if she cried he would cut her fingers off one by one and feed them to the cows.

The day they took her they had tied her feet and hands together but not very tight. They had also stuffed a dirty smelly rag into her mouth and kept her in a hut with no windows. It had been very dark inside but she'd known there were people outside. She could hear them moving about and talking. Then the next day, the pretty woman had come. She told the other men to untie her and had removed the rag from her mouth. She gave Naa Teiki some water to drink and allowed Naa to urinate in the bushes but Naa had been so frightened of snakes that she had peed standing up and had wetted herself. The woman had told her that they were going on a short journey and she would soon see her parents again.

Naa Teiki did not believe her. Why would they make her hide in this truck and why did they whisper when they talked? Why did they always travel at night when it was too dark to see anything? She whimpered and felt the tears slide down her face. She wanted to see Mummy and Daddy and her baby brother again. She wanted to get off this truck and sleep in her own bed. She did not like these people. She was afraid of them.

She froze as she felt a cow come near and nuzzle the blanket. Presently she felt a warm smelly stream of fluid seep through the blanket and trickle down her arm. Terrified she screamed and let out a stream of urine herself. Apart from the cows in the trailer there was no one to hear her. Even Jagger who was driving and the pretty woman who had fallen asleep did not hear her as they drove on the dry dusty road.

CHAPTER FOUR
New Friends When All Seemed Lost

It was early morning when the truck finally came to a stop. Naa Teiki still lay huddled under the blankets. She heard someone climb onto the truck and she felt herself being lifted up. She was transferred quickly into the backseat of another car and they drove off again into the night. It took some time for her eyes to adjust to the darkness but soon she made out the forms of Nancy, Jagger and another man. Jagger was driving and the other man sat beside him in front. The man made Jagger stop the car then he removed the blanket and looked her over critically. He turned her around and studied her some more. He wrinkled his nose when he caught wind of her smell. A look of disgust crossed his face.

"Do you wet your bed when you sleep?"

Naa was too terrified to speak. He didn't have an ugly scar like Jagger but he looked very mean.

"She's perfect," he told Nancy and Jagger who had been holding their breaths, "apart from the bedwetting. You did well. We'll keep her for a month or so till it is safe to move her out."

Naa Teiki was glad to be away from the cows but she was still afraid. The car slowed down. Ahead of them was a road block. Naa could see police men shining their torch lights into the cars ahead of them.

"Drat, you should have used another road." The man sitting beside Jagger said. Jagger mumbled something. The man turned and looked at Naa. "Pretend to sleep and if the police men wake you up, say this woman is your mother and we are your uncles. Do you understand?"

Naa nodded. Nancy made Naa put her head in her lap then she covered her with the smelly blankets and they both pretended to sleep.

Naa felt the car stop. She felt a light beam directed at her and she closed her eyes shut. She heard the policeman talk to the big man in front but she couldn't hear what they said. She began to tremble but felt the woman's hand on her back, stroking her. Then she felt the car pick up speed and they drove away. They stopped again and the man in front alighted.

"You better get moving before daylight ," he said and handed over a set of keys to Jagger and walked into the darkness. Nancy moved into the front beside Jagger.

"Where are we going?" Naa Teiki asked. She was relieved that the big man was gone.

"You'll know soon enough," the woman said and refused to answer any more questions Naa asked. Naa remained quiet. She was tired, cold and hungry.

It was still dark when they drove to a house or rather half of a house. Part of the building was in ruins and the other half didn't look any better. Naa could smell ripe mangoes but she couldn't see much of anything. Nancy and Jagger led her inside. There were cobwebs everywhere and Naa screamed when a spider landed on her neck. Jagger quickly covered her mouth with his hand.

They went up a flight of very rickety stairs that creaked with every step they took. Then the woman took out a bunch of keys and opened a door. She pushed Naa inside and they both followed and locked it behind them.

They had entered a room with four bunk beds. The room was clean and did not have the stuffy smell of the rest of the house. There was neither dust nor cobwebs. There were six children in the room. Naa Teiki blinked in surprise.

"Adoley" Jagger called out.

A girl about fourteen years approached him. He thrust Naa Teiki at her. "See that she gets a bath and some food to eat." Adoley said nothing but she put a comforting arm around Naa Teiki. After giving some more instructions, Jagger and Nancy left.

Adoley knelt down and wiped the tears off Naa Teiki's face. "We'll take good care of you; you'll be safe with us." For the first time since she'd been kidnapped Naa Teiki felt safe. She smiled at the big girl.

CHAPTER FIVE
Neighbours At Last!

Koku had gone to his secret garden, up on the hill. His bean seedlings were sprouting. In a matter of weeks, he'd have enough beans to feed his family. Mr. Danso, the agricultural science teacher had given him some cabbage seeds as well but those had not broken through the soil yet. Some green tomatoes and pepper hung from their branches. He was careful to prune the branches so that the fruits would have enough nutrients to grow. He also had cocoyam but those were easy to grow. Maybe he could plant onions next time. He had never tried onions before. He wondered how they would do.

He was lost deep in thought as he made his way down the hill. As predicted, his father had not been happy with his grades. "How do you hope to enter a good senior high school when you can't even get aggregate 6?" His father had asked. "Don't you want to go to a good school like Sena?" He had quickly arranged for a tutor for Koku. The man came three times a week, from nine to eleven am. The man taught him English and Mathematics. His father had also added a new rule; Koku could only play his computer games for an hour each day. He was to spend every spare time he had to improve his vocabulary by reading the newspaper or by reading books.

He hoped his father never found out that he had his own garden. "Why do you want to be a farmer?" His father had asked him this question a million times. "Be an engineer, or a lawyer or a medical doctor." His father had suggested. But Koku didn't like any of those things. He had tried explaining to his father that he loved watching things grow. It was like magic. You put a tiny seed in the ground. Give it some water from time to time and in a little while you have fruit and more seeds in the fruit. His father had snorted and chuckled angrily at his explanation then said "no son of mine will be a farmer" and stormed out of the room.

Two big trucks drove by him startling him out of his reverie. He caught a glimpse of pieces of furniture and a bicycle in one of the trucks. He chased the trucks down the road to the newly completed house and sat down to watch from a distance as four big men got down and began offloading the furniture. Apart from the men, there was no one else in sight. He plucked a blade of grass and began nibbling it. How he hoped this new family had children his age. He was tired of always being on his own and having no one to play with. Ami his younger sister always wanted to play with her dolls. She would not play football or chase lizards or swim in the little pond by their house. She was such a bore. His closest friend from school, Manuel, lived a long distance away and Mama did not like having him walk there on his own and she was always too busy to take him as often as he would have liked.

"This was the trouble with this neighbourhood," he thought to himself while kicking a stone. But his Father liked it here. He called it his little "piece of peace." Koku knew by now that was a pun. Daddy had said it so many times that if he got asked in his sleep to give an example of a pun, he could without waking up. Many new houses were being constructed but he was tired of exploring the area and watching the construction workers. He wished there was someone with whom he could kick a ball. He missed his old home and the friends he had left in Tema. He missed the busy roads and the fast cars. He missed all the people. It had been over two years since they moved here but Koku still couldn't think of Afienya as home. Home would always be Tema and the single room he'd shared with his two sisters. However, he was glad that he had his own room here and did not have to share it. A mosquito bit him and he got up. It was getting late. He had to go home or else Mama would worry.

A saloon car drove quickly past him when he got to his gate. The family had arrived. He felt a quiver of excitement and rushed into the house.

"Mama! Mama! The new people have come! The new people have come!" He cried rushing into the kitchen and nearly tripping over Ami, who sat on the kitchen floor playing with her doll, Yaayaa, and the cat.

"Ami, pack your toys I could have fallen down" he said annoyed. Ami ignored him. She was still angry that he had refused to let her tag along for the walk. Ami was five years old and anytime he took her with him she always said she was tired and refused to walk when it was time to come back home. The last time, he had had to carry her all the way home.

"Which new people?" his mother asked. She was busy stirring the thick creamy mixture that in a few minutes would harden into the *banku* that Koku loved so much. He could see crabs, pieces of fish and *wele* swimming in the okra soup that was bubbling away furiously on one of the burners of the gas stove.

"Our new neighbours, those down the road from us. I saw the truck that brought their things and their car just passed in front of our gate. Can we go and greet them?" he asked looking hopefully at his mother. He tried to pilfer a piece of fish from the soup but his mother smacked his hand.

"It's late Koku; they must be tired from travelling all day," Mama said looking at the clock, "besides supper is almost ready. Go and bath and bath Ami for me. Supper should be ready by the time you finish."

His mother was right Koku thought. His stomach rumbled and another whiff of the appetising aroma of the soup made him shelf the thought of visiting the new neighbours. He hoped Mama would give him two pieces of *wele*, if not maybe he could ask Ami to give him hers. She hardly ever chewed it and ended up giving it either back to his mother or to the cat. Maybe she'd agree to trade part of his fish for her *wele*.

He reached down to take Ami's hand but she snatched it out of his. "I can bath myself" she said angrily and strode to the bathroom. Koku looked to his mother for help. Mama was smiling, "you should play with her sometimes."

Koku shook his head. This was a bad start. There was no way Ami was going to give him her piece of *wele*.

CHAPTER SIX

The Strange Boy

"**M**ama, can we go now?" Koku asked eager to get going. His tutor had already left. Koku had had to write two essays and complete twenty similes. There should be one that says 'as late as Mama' he thought to himself. His mother was always late which made his father, who couldn't tolerate lateness and laziness, as mad as a hatter.

It had been two whole days since the new people had come. Mama had said the new family needed time to settle and unpack their things before they started having visitors. Yesterday, she had said they would go today. Today she had said this afternoon. And now she was taking forever to get Ami ready.

He'd passed in front of the house twice already. Yesterday evening and early this morning. But the wall was high and he had not been able to see anything. How he wished the new family had a boy his age he could play with.

They finally came out. Ami looked neat and clean in a white dress. It was one of her old ones. Mama said it was too old to use for church but not old enough to be worn in the house. Mama herself wore a yellow and brown battick *kaba* and *slit*. Mama took one look at him and shook her head. Koku knew what was coming next. "Go and change that shirt, wash your face, comb your hair and wash the dust from your feet." Koku groaned but he did as his mother said rushing into the bathroom to splash his face with cold water and to comb his hair. Then he changed his shirt, wiped his feet with a rag and hurried back. He didn't have a clean handkerchief so he refolded the old one he had in his pocket so that the dirty side would not show. They walked down the street together. Ami run ahead of them to pick wild flowers growing by the roadside.

"*Agoo*" Mama called out when they got to the new neighbour's gate. They waited. No one came to the gate. "*Agoo*," she called out again. Presently, a boy about Koku's age came to the gate. He was dressed in shorts and a green t-shirt. Koku smiled broadly. Thank God, they had a son. Mama made the introductions and the boy led them inside and offered them seats on the veranda. They had nice bamboo chairs but there were boxes everywhere. The boy disappeared inside to get his mother.

Koku looked around; one part of the compound was covered with weeds. Someone had begun weeding but had not quite finished it. There were a few empty flower pots stacked up by one of the walls. Empty boxes and pieces of paper were strewn all over the compound. Koku spied not one but two bicycles near the garage. He was very pleased; maybe the boy could teach him to ride. He had never ridden a bicycle before.

Ami struggled to climb one of the chairs. It was a rocking chair and when Mama said she should sit in another chair she refused. Once she succeeded in getting settled in, she made herself comfortable and stuck her fingers into her mouth and began sucking vigorously as the chair rocked to and fro.

As Mama was scolding her the boy came out again, a box in his hand. He had changed his t-shirt. He wore a red one now. He looked surprised to see them on the veranda. He was so surprised that he screamed and dropped the box he was carrying. There was the sound of glass breaking as the box hit the floor. He rushed back into the house.

Koku turned to look at Mama who looked as surprised as he did. Ami's mouth hung open. She couldn't decide whether to put her fingers back into her mouth or not.

"I think we should leave," Mama whispered to Koku picking Ami up.

"Yes, let's leave." Koku whispered back. What a strange boy, he thought not sure if he still wanted to be friends with him or not. They stepped over the box the boy had dropped. Careful not to step on any of the broken bits of glass and made their way hurriedly to the gate casting nervous glances behind them in case any more members of this strange new family came out.

CHAPTER SEVEN

Twins!

When they got to the gate, a woman called out to them. The boy stood behind her, a confused look on his face. He looked exactly like the woman and he had changed back into the green t-shirt. "That must be his mother," Mama whispered. The woman was short and round. The boy was taller than her. She pulled out a dirty handkerchief and wiped her face and neck. Her hair peeked out from under a scarf. She must have been dusting something indoors for traces of dust were on the scarf and the part of her hair that was exposed. She broke into a smile which made her eyes twinkle and asked, "Are you leaving already? Do come back, we don't know anyone at all in this town."

Mama looked at Koku who was shaking his head. Though she looked harmless they couldn't be so sure if she was really any different from her son. "We ... uh..." Mama began, "we thought we'd come by later, seeing how busy you are......"

"Nonsense," the woman said walking briskly to the gate and closing it firmly behind her. She shepherded them back towards the veranda, talking nonstop the whole time about how Mama had come exactly at the right moment and how she needed a female perspective on where to put certain pieces of furniture in the house. She seemed to notice the broken glass on the floor for the first time and turned to look at the boy who was still behind her.

"When did this happen?" She asked. "I keep telling you to be careful with the boxes, now see what you have done." Though she sounded angry, she didn't even have a frown on her face.

"It wasn't me," the boy protested. Koku looked at Mama. The boy was lying. Hadn't they both seen him drop that box and rush back inside?

"Never mind, get a broom and clear this mess before someone cuts themselves." She turned back to Mama smiling and commented on the beautiful style of Mama's *kaba* and *slit* . Mama smiled proudly and told her she had sewn it herself. Koku could see the woman was impressed and he didn't have to be a clairvoyant to know Mama had just gotten another customer.

The boy was about to enter the house when another boy came out holding a broom and a dustpan. The new boy was in a red t-shirt.

Mama and Koku looked at each other again in surprise. The boys were twins! Realizing their mistake Mama and Koku burst out laughing. Then Mama recounted the story saying how they had been alarmed. Everyone laughed including the twin boys and even Ami. The woman introduced herself as Agnes Darko. She said they were to call her Auntie Aggie. The boys were Yaw Atta Panyin Darko and Yaw Atta Kakra Darko. Panyin and Kakra for short. Kakra, the twin in the green t-shirt, had been weeding when they knocked on the gate. He had met them and gone in to call his mother. Panyin was the other twin in the red t-shirt. He had not known they had visitors and had been frightened when he saw them on the veranda causing him to drop the box he'd been carrying.

"One of the drivers who brought our things told us there was a haunted house. He said some people had seen ghosts walking on the compound and when I came out and saw you I was a little surprised..." Panyin said somewhat sheepishly.

Mama chuckled and said, "Ah! So you've heard about the haunted house already, it was the very first story we were told when we also moved here."

"Is it truly haunted?" he asked again with a worried look.

"People claim sometimes they hear children crying and see lights blinking in the windows but I haven't been near that house and I don't plan on going anywhere it." Mama said with a firm shake of her head.

Auntie Aggie wanted a second opinion so she invited Mama into the house. Ami followed them inside though no one had invited her in. They left the three boys outside to get acquainted much to Koku's delight.

CHAPTER EIGHT

Almost A Family

Adoley watched as the latest newcomer to their little group tossed and turned in her sleep. She had already been here for a week. This girl was different; she wasn't from the streets like the rest of them. She wore good clothes and good shoes and she spoke good English, she was more like Sherif and Malik. She had not been able to get much out of the girl apart from her name, the name of her neighbourhood and the name of her school. Adoley had neither heard of the neighbourhood nor the school.

Jagger and Nancy treated her differently as well. They had brought clean blankets and more food. She'd overheard Jagger telling Nancy that by the end of the month all the children would be sent away. She knew it was up to her to find a way to get them out. She was the oldest. It was her responsibility. But though she'd searched and searched there was no way out of the room except through the door which was locked. All the windows had been painted black and barred with pieces of wood. Holes had been made for ventilation but those were so small that they could only wiggle three fingers through. She peeped through one of the ventilation holes. Nothing.

Mawuga woke up and came to sit by her side.

"Any luck?" he asked.

Adoley shook her head. "No, there was no moon; I wouldn't even have been able to tell if someone came close."

Mawuga rubbed his face with the back of his hand, stifled a yawn and sat by her side. He looked through one hole. Their view of the outside compound was partly obscured by a huge mango tree. The children had hoped they could draw the attention of a passerby but for the one month that Adoley had been in the house, the only ones who came and went were Jagger and Nancy. Absentmindedly Adoley rubbed the scar on her arm

"Do you sometimes wonder where you'd be if we hadn't been caught and brought here?" Mawuga asked quietly.

Adoley snorted. "I don't wonder, I know I'd be dead. My aunt would surely have killed me if I hadn't run away. Coming to Accra was the wisest thing I ever did." She rolled back the sleeve of the shirt she wore. "See this scar here?" she asked Mawuga. He nodded. "This was what finally made me leave."

"What happened?" he asked.

"I come from a large family," Adoley began. "I have..." she paused to count "six sisters and three brothers, all younger than me. My parents are both farmers and sometimes when it doesn't rain on time, feeding us becomes difficult. Last two years my aunt came to the village and begged my parents to let me come and live with her. She said she'd send me to JHS and pay my fees and afterwards I'd learn a trade, maybe hairdressing or sewing. My parents were overjoyed, so was I."

One by one all the other children woke up and drew closer to Adoley.

"What happened next?" Kwame Joe asked stretching and opening his mouth in a big yawn. He had joined them two weeks ago and was still getting used to being confined in the stuffy room.

"We lived in Madina. Initially, my aunt was nice and I started school but then she said the school fees were too expensive and I was withdrawn. So I started selling eggs by the roadside. But she kept saying I was stealing her money and began beating me. She refused to give me food as well. One night she misplaced her purse but she said I'd stolen it. To make me confess, she heated an iron and put it on my arm but for the timely intervention of a neighbour I don't know what else she would have done. That night I run away from the house and came to Accra Central, I started selling pure water on the streets till I met Jagger. He said he owned a restaurant and would pay me good money to be a waitress. I agreed and this is where he brought me."

"Jagger brought you to be our mother, Faustie said climbing into Adoley's lap and you're the best mother we ever had." Faustie was a little older than Naa Teiki but she was so malnourished she looked younger than her. Her poor family had sold her outright to Jagger and Nancy.

"Will they kill us and use our body parts for rituals?" Sherif asked Adoley. He lay coiled up on the bed beside his brother, Malik, who had never spoken a word since they'd been captured and brought there.

Adoley looked round the faces of the children. She read pure unadulterated fear in each face. She smiled and tried to cheer them up. It wouldn't do to have them discover she was as anxious as they were. She wasn't sure exactly where Jagger and Nancy would be sending them to but wherever it was, she knew for sure, it wouldn't be pleasant.

"No, I don't think so. Why would they bring us all this food, if they were going to kill us?"

The children nodded their agreement and for the time being the fear was dispelled. "Maybe they want to find nice families for us. Then we'll have our own parents and our beds. Our new parents will be nice and they'll send us to school and they'll throw parties for us on our birthdays." Faustie said excitedly.

Not everyone agreed with Faustie. "I like my own parents; I just want to go home." Sherif said. He and Malik had been abducted on their way home from school. The idea of new parents appealed to Faustie, Mawuga and Kwame Joe who had been sleeping on the streets but the others had relatives they missed and wanted to get back to.

"She didn't cry last night." Mawuga said looking at Naa Teiki who was the only one still asleep. He peeped through the ventilation hole. "I wish we could get some of those mangoes, they look so juicy." That started a discussion on which region in Ghana the juiciest mangoes came from.

Adoley watched them with mixed feelings. They had come to replace the brothers and sisters she had left behind in her village but there was absolutely nothing she could do to protect them from Jagger and Nancy and their wicked plans.

CHAPTER NINE

Settling Down

"You'll both be in my class." Koku told the twins one morning. They were also thirteen years old. The twins were identical and it took some time before he could tell them apart. There was no distinguishing feature you could look out for and in the beginning it had been difficult. The twins had not made it easier, sometimes responding to the same name or at other times pretending not to be the one being addressed. They never dressed alike though. Koku even doubted if they had the same items of clothing.

Mama and Ami still had a hard time telling them apart. But the twins were respectful and well behaved before Mama and never tried pulling any tricks on her. They also both liked Ami and didn't mind when she followed them around and asked all kinds of annoying questions. Panyin even sometimes joined her play with her dolls. He made up stories involving the dolls and pussy cat much to Ami's delight. Koku could only look on with chagrin. He couldn't imagine what his friends in school would think if they found out Panyin played with Ami and her dolls. He could only hope they would never find out.

Koku was helping them weed a part of the compound Auntie Aggie wanted to use to plant vegetables. Koku had immersed himself completely in the project. The icing on the cake had been when she said he could have his own vegetable bed in their yard. He'd been ecstatic. He had been looking for a reason to come to see the twins everyday and Auntie Aggie had provided him with one. She had cleared it with his parents. His Father had not been thrilled with the idea of encouraging him to grow things but Auntie Aggie, who could be very persuasive when she wanted, had had her way.

The twins' house now had a lived- in feel to it though the smell of fresh paint still lingered. The boys shared a big room but had not finished unpacking their belongings. It looked like a pig sty but their parents had given up on asking them to tidy up. Koku had promised to show them around the neighbourhood, not that there was much of anything to be seen but he thought they might like the pond and they *had* promised to teach him to ride a bicycle. He was eager to get started. Auntie Aggie had promised that as soon as they finished with the weeding they could go out and explore.

"I'm sure we'll like it" Kakra said. "Panyin is the more studious one, can you believe, last semester he had 2's in all his subjects?" Kakra said regarding his brother with respect and awe. "He had aggregate 12! He's going to be a medical doctor and invent the cure for cancer." The brothers assumed Koku's look of shock was surprise at Panyin's outstanding performance.

"Me, I'm going to be a footballer." Kakra said dribbling an imaginary ball around their feet. "I had aggregate 15," he announced. "Not bad for a footballer, eh?"

"What did your Father say?" Koku asked with an incredulous expression on his face.

"About what?" the twins asked in unison, looking confused.

"About both your grades and your profession?" he said looking pointedly at Kakra.

"Nothing." Kakra said shrugging his shoulders. "He knows I'll be the next Michael Essien but I will not play for Chelsea. I'll play for United."

Koku didn't know what to think. He had aggregate 9 and was having extra tuition! It was unbelievable! He would have given anything at that point to exchange fathers.

"So what do you do all day?" Kakra asked once they'd finished weeding. They lay on their backs in the shade of an Indian almond tree. They still had to collect all the rubbish and burn it.

"I have a teacher who comes to help me with my Maths and English. I didn't do too well in those subjects and my Father wasn't very happy." Koku confessed.

"Why? what aggregate did you get?" Kakra asked. He couldn't imagine having to study during the holidays.

"Aggregate 9."

"9!" Both boys exclaimed sitting up and looking at Koku in astonishment. Their mouths hung open for a full minute. "Wow! I have never gotten a single digit aggregate before." Panyin said looking at him with deference. Kakra just kept repeating "9, 9, 9..." It was the only thing he said for a while.

Koku laughed when he imagined the look on their faces if they ever got to see Manuel's report card.

"When does your teacher come? Panyin asked after some-time.

"In the mornings and it's three times a week. But I have to read the newspaper every morning. Father says it's to help me with my English. After that I'm free to do what I like, sometimes I play video games but Mama only lets me play for an hour a day. Sometimes I visit Manuel and we play football but mostly I just go for walks."

"We'd like to join you for your studies" Panyin said. Kakra who had been chanting "9, 9, 9..." like a mantra stopped suddenly and asked in surprise "we would?"

"Yes we would," Panyin said "we don't want to be last in our new school." Kakra groaned and lay back on the grass.

"We'll tell our parents we want to, that's if you don't mind sharing your tutor." Panyin told Koku.

"Sure, I'd like that." In a bid to change the subject he asked, "did you hear about that little girl who was kidnapped?"

That got Kakra's attention. "We saw her parents on the TV. They looked really sad. Imagine having all the money in the world and still not being able to help your daughter."

"Mama is so scared she doesn't let Ami out of her sight these days. What I don't understand is that why they haven't asked for a ransom if they are kidnappers?" Koku said.

"Maybe they don't want the money. Maybe they'll use her for rituals." Kakra said saying the one thing they were all thinking but afraid to voice.

"I hope the police find her soon." Panyin said getting up and dusting his shorts. "Come on, let's finish collecting the rubbish. It looks like it would rain tonight."

CHAPTER TEN
Exploring Afienya

Early the next morning the twins were at Koku's house. Their father, Mr. Darko, had spoken to Mr. Amegatsey who had spoken to the tutor and everything had been settled nicely. They joined him for the session with the tutor. Then they played hide and seek with Ami while he read through the morning paper, wrote down new words he didn't know and found out their meanings in the dictionary. It was almost lunch time when he finished.

Mama had just finished frying hot plantain and the boys drooled as she ladled out hot spoonfuls of bean stew dripping with red palm oil. They did not have to be coaxed to eat. Kakra who was always hungry and had an appetite of a horse had a second helping. Koku had never seen anyone eat as much as him. Mama gave them slices of pineapple for dessert. They had to wait for Ami to fall asleep before silently creeping out of the house. She knew they were planning on going exploring and she very much wanted to go but Koku didn't want her with them.

Koku took them on a short tour of the inhabited part of the neighbourhood. There wasn't much to see. There were just a couple of houses with people whose children were in the universities, no 'young families' like his father would say. There was a lot of arable land. Most people had large maize and cassava farms.

Finally, he took them to his most favourite, most secret, most special spot in the whole area. It was on a little steep hill which overlooked the whole area. The climb up was tiring and by the time they got to the summit, the twins were out of breath. However, the view was breathtaking and right at the top of the hill was a little pond filled with the clearest cleanest water the twins had ever seen. The twins admired Koku's vegetables but he could see they were just being polite and were not really into gardening. He didn't mind at all. He was just happy that at last he could discuss his garden with someone. The twins gaped at the scenery. The rustic countryside lay spread out like a map. They could make out the main road. The vehicles looked like toys. They spotted some cows in one field. They looked like ants.

"I didn't think I could make it up here." Panyin said still gasping for breath. "But now that I'm up here, I don't think, I want to go down."

"It's really a beautiful place. Is that our house there?" Kakra asked pointing into the distance. Panyin turned to where he was pointing. "It is, isn't it Koku?"

"Yes," Koku answered, "and that's my house. That white tower there is our school and the church is that one there with a cross, there's the police station over there and the market."

"I didn't know so many people were putting up houses here," Kakra said. "Just look at the number of uncompleted buildings.

Soon there'll be a lot of people here. Maybe we might even get enough boys for a proper football match."

"I think, that one would be a hotel," Koku said pointing to a huge building. "And there is the haunted house."

"Are there ghosts there?" Panyin asked his eyes growing wide.

"I don't really know the story behind it but some people say at night they hear people there and yet no one lives there." Koku said.

"Can we go and check it out?" Kakra asked. His brother groaned in despair.

"I haven't been there before." Koku didn't want to sound like a coward but he didn't want to be mixed up with haunted houses and ghosts. "Come on; let's go for a quick swim." He said removing his shirt and sprinting towards the cool refreshing waters of the pond. He made a big splash as he dove inside.

The twins jumped in as well and they began to splash each other relishing the feel of the cold water in the hot weather. The pond wasn't deep. When they stood up, their feet touched the gravels at the bottom. When they grew tired of splashing they got out of the water and lay down on the dry grass and made out shapes in the clouds.

"See, that one looks like a man's head." Panyin said pointing.

"That one's like a crab"

"No, it's like an umbrella."

Kakra's stomach rumbled. "I'm hungry, he announced, let's get going." The others got up and put on their shirts. It was getting late. They helped Koku water his plants then they raced down the steep hill promising to meet again the next morning.

"See you tomorrow," they called out to each other.

CHAPTER ELEVEN

The Clean Up

As it turned out the boys could not go exploring the haunted house the next day or the day after. Koku's father had asked Koku to clean out his sister's room. Sena was coming home the next day and Ami's toys and books were strewn all over the room they shared. Sena's bed was buried under a pile of stuffed animals. Ami stood looking from the doorway. Her little arms crossed over her chest, disapproval written all over her face.

"Where should I put these?" he asked. She pointed to her bed which looked no better.

"Then where will you sleep?"

She climbed onto the bed and created space.

"Why must they all be on your bed anyway?" He asked.

"So that I can talk to them." She replied.

Koku shook his head but the more he thought about it the more he understood Ami. At least he now had friends to talk to and to play with, Ami had no one her age to play with and she wasn't allowed out of the house on her own. She must really be lonely he thought. He hadn't been a very good big brother, even the twins played with her but he shunned her completely. He went to Mama and asked to borrow one of her big cane baskets. He placed it at the foot of Ami's bed and began sorting through the toys. He made two piles, one pile was for good toys and the other was for toys missing body parts of which there were several. Most of the toys had been passed down from Sena to him and from him to Ami. Some of them brought back memories to him and he smiled as he remembered fighting with Sena over them when they were both younger.

Ami looked on in horror as the pile with the disabled body parts kept growing bigger and bigger. "What are you doing?" She finally demanded, "Will you throw them away?" The tone of her voice made him wary. She looked like she was about to cry.

"No, I'll put these ones," he indicated the pile with the missing body parts, "at the bottom of the basket and these ones will be on top. But they'll all be here so you can take them whenever you need them."

Satisfied with that explanation she helped him put the toys into the cane basket. Then they arranged her books on the shelf along with her crayons and colour pencils. They taped pictures she'd drawn on her side of the bedroom. "I drew a picture for Sena." She said.

"A picture?"

She rummaged through her school bag and produced a very crumpled piece of paper. She placed it on the table and straightened the wrinkles out with her hand. It showed five asymmetrical people. Two big ones and three smaller ones and a slightly rectangular object. "This is Daddy, Mama, Sena, you and me and this" she pointed to the rectangular object "is the cat." She had drawn their family. She looked up at him expectantly.

"It's very pretty."

She looked very pleased with herself. "It's so that Sena would not miss us too much when she's in school."

Koku was surprised that Ami would be that perceptive. "I'll draw one for you too when you go." She said mistaking his look for sadness that she hadn't drawn a picture for him.

"I'll like that very much." He said. She beamed at him.

"Let's put that on the wall by Sena's bed so she'll see it each night before she sleeps and in the morning when she wakes up."

"Ok," she said happily and run to Sena's bed with the picture.

Unbidden the image of the little kidnapped girl came to Koku's mind. He shuddered. He wouldn't want anything to happen to Ami. She could be annoying but most of the time she was sweet. As he taped the picture to the wall he resolved to spend more time with her. That afternoon after lunch, she read to him from her big picture book. She was very proud of herself though she had to follow the words with her fingers. She read well. Koku praised her. Then he told her Ananse stories and they napped together on the veranda. When they woke, they played hopscotch. Koku made her win each time and she was thrilled. That night she gave him her piece of *wele* without him asking for it.

CHAPTER TWELVE

A History Lesson

The next day, Daddy drove them to Cape Coast where Sena's school was. They had had to set off very early. The twins had asked to come along, having never been to the Central Region. They all slept throughout the journey.

Sena was the only one in front of her dormitory when they got there. She refused to hug her father and ignored her siblings totally. She mumbled a greeting to the twins. Koku was very disappointed. He had talked so much about his sister, who had had aggregate 6 and 10 ones and 90% in all the subjects, to the twins and now she wouldn't even be nice and say 'hello' properly.

"Daddy I'm a big girl, you shouldn't have come for me. I could have come home on my own." She said picking up her bag and sitting in the car. She was angry and sullen and wouldn't talk to anyone.

"It's a long journey, your Mother and I didn't want you making it on your own, maybe next time." Daddy suggested.

"I'm not a baby," she said as she sat in front beside her father. She fell asleep when they began the journey home. Koku could see that Daddy was not happy but maybe he didn't want to make a scene in front of the twins. The twins much to their credit said nothing about her behaviour and they took turns in tickling Ami and telling funny stories. Daddy pointed out the Cape Coast Castle to them as they passed in front of it and because Koku, the twins and Ami begged and begged he turned the car round and took them to the castle. Sena wouldn't join them. She said she'd already been to the castle on a school trip. Koku was relieved; he didn't want her spoiling the atmosphere with her bad mood.

Daddy paid the entrance fee at the castle and they were taken on a tour. Koku was awed by the size of the castle. True, the white paint was peeling in areas and there was a slight musty smell to the place but what did he expect, considering it was over three hundred years old? They were the only ones there and the tour guide, Mr. Ankamah, took them around.

First, he showed them a documentary showing the origins of the castle and a history of the slave trade. Then he took them to the museum where the shackles that were put around the necks, wrists and ankles of the slaves were kept. They also had on display guns, gold dust, bows, arrows, stools, cloth and various pictures of the early slaves, the chiefs, the colonial masters and slave ships. One picture showed the cargo compartment of a merchant ship where slaves were arranged like sardines in a tin. The caption beneath it said each ship took between two hundred to two hundred and fifty slaves. Sometimes the slaves were arranged in two rows, one above the other and packed so close together that there was no room to move. The tour guide told them that slave raiders laid ambush in the forests and sometimes they captured the inhabitants of entire villages. Sometimes the chiefs and family heads sold criminals to the raiders.

Next, they went into the dungeons. Mr. Ankamah said when slaves were captured they were kept in the dungeons till the cargo ships came for them. Sometimes they were kept there for months. The dungeons were dark and gloomy and the air was musty. Ami gripped Daddy's hand and held him tight. Daddy picked her up and stroked her back. She was right to be afraid Koku thought, he imagined what it would have been like to have been captured and brought here. He imagined being separated from his parents, his sisters and friends forever. It was not a pleasant thought.

They came out of the dungeons into the bright sunlight and looked out to the sea. Koku imagined being carried across it in a big ship. Lying flat on his back. Not having enough space to stretch or turn around. Seeing the sunlight only through slits in the wall. Defecating and urinating in the same place in which you slept. Being shackled to a dead body. Watching as dead people were thrown overboard into the seas. Arriving in a strange country. Being exhibited and sold like pigs in a market place. Learning a new language, being branded with a red hot iron and having to work as hard as a donkey. Never ever getting to see the land where you born. He shivered in the warm sunlight and drew his arms around himself.

"I'm glad slavery is over," he said speaking his thoughts aloud.

"But it's not!" Mr. Ankamah exclaimed looking at him in surprise. "Even right now as we speak we still have people in slavery."

"But we are a free independent country," Panyin challenged.

"That's right, we rule ourselves, and we don't have colonial masters anymore." Kakra added.

Mr. Ankamah sighed and said "Modern day slaves are not held in dungeons and shipped to Europe and the Americas, no, they are trafficked."

They looked at him confused. Ami was still in Daddy's arms. She had stuck a finger into her mouth and was sucking. Koku had come to realize she only sucked her fingers when she was scared.

Mr. Ankamah continued, "Girls and boys as young as six are sometimes taken from desperately poor homes, others are snatched off the streets and placed as domestic workers with strangers in the city. Many go willingly, but some are tricked. They are taken to a witch doctor, sworn to secrecy and made to believe if they attempt running away, they will die. In return, they are promised an education. In reality, they are often beaten, fed on leftovers, forced to work long hours and forbidden to go to school. Other children are sent to work in quarries or plantations, some dive into the deep seas to lay traps for fish while older fishermen instruct them from canoes. Some are even trafficked for ritual purposes and end up dead. Other children are trafficked for work outside the country. So you see slavery is still very much a part of our society."

The young boys nodded solemnly digesting this new bit of information. "It is ironic that even after the European slave masters had gone, we ourselves have picked up the whips and continue to enslave our brothers and sisters." Mr. Amegatsey said thoughtfully.

It's a different thing learning about slavery from a textbook and a different thing seeing the slave castle with your own eyes Koku thought as they thanked, waved 'goodbye' to Mr. Ankamah and made their way back to the car park where Sena was still asleep in the car.

CHAPTER THIRTEEN

A Different Sena

Sena's bad mood lasted the whole day. When they got home she ripped off the picture Ami had drawn for her from her wall. She balled it up and threw it into the waste paper basket. That made Ami sad and she started crying.

Her parents couldn't understand what was wrong with her. Then Daddy got angry and scolded her. She started crying and went to her room as well. Though Mama had cooked jollof rice with big pieces of fried chicken, no one had much of an appetite. In the evening, Sena apologized to Ami and to her parents. Ami who had retrieved her picture from the waste paper basket refused to give it back to her. She gave it to Koku instead who taped it to his wall.

In the ensuing days, Sena did her chores as was expected of her. She also had no friends in the area and spent most of her time on the phone with her friends or on the internet. Since she did not have a problem with her grades she had no time restrictions on her computer use. In fact, after a few days, she was back to her normal self and her parents were glad. They both agreed it was probably the change of environment that had accounted for her strange behaviour. Raising a teenager was not easy.

Koku was confused by his sister's mood swings. Sometimes after spending hours on the internet and chatting with her friends she'd be so happy. On these days she could be heard humming a tune to herself as she tidied up the kitchen after supper. Sometimes she even helped Ami with her reading and joined her to play with dolls.

On other days she looked like she was waiting for something and sat behind the computer the whole day. On those days she didn't talk to anyone and kept to herself. Most of the time, she'd stick earphones into her ears and listen to music. That was always a sign for everyone to stay as far away from her as possible.

Koku didn't see how the same internet could make her both happy and sad. All he was allowed to use the internet for was to send and receive mail from his friends. His father had his password. If he had to use it for homework, his father sat by his side and they did it together. Sena on the other hand could do as she pleased without supervision. As far as he could tell all she did on the computer was watch pictures her friends had put up and comment on them.

One day Sena was using the computer when she got a phone call. She was away for thirty minutes. Mama came into the room, a tape measure around her neck; she was looking for her marking chalk which Ami had been playing with. "Put off that thing if no one is using it." Mama said referring to the computer.

Koku was looking for the meaning of new words with his dictionary. He'd just finished reading the newspaper. He hesitated. He went to check on Sena she was still on the phone with her friend. She didn't look like she'd be finished anytime soon. He went back to the computer and was about to close the window when he stopped. Sena had been chatting with someone called Big Daddy. It appeared she called herself Anes. She could have chosen a better name Koku thought; anyone could see Anes was an anagram. It was Sena spelt backwards. He didn't mean to but he found himself reading:

Big Daddy: I hope things are better at home now

What exactly had Sena told this person to make him question how conditions in home were? Koku wondered:

Anes: It could be better.

Big Daddy: I would really like to see you.

Anes: I already sent you a picture.

Big Daddy: I meant in person, the sooner the better.
You are very beautiful.

Anes: Thank you but how will we meet?

Big Daddy: Don't your parents go to work?

Anes: Only my Dad does, my Mom sews in the house.

Big Daddy: I'll call you later tonight.
I miss you already.

Anes: ok, I miss you too.

Koku was still reading when he heard Sena coming back. He hurried back to his seat and opened the dictionary. He was sweating so much, he thought Sena would notice but she didn't. She closed the page, switched off the computer and went into the kitchen for a drink.

CHAPTER FOURTEEN

A Strange Tale

The next day, after their lessons, the boys went back to the twins' house. A young man was digging out stumps from the weeded part of the compound. His name was Bro. Ebo he did odd jobs in the neighbourhood and Koku knew him well. He wore dirty jeans cut off at the knee. He sang a tune to himself.

My sweetie
My sugar
Oh yes

At the end of each line he brought the pickaxe down. It struck the earth around the root, loosening it up a bit. It was hard work and sweat run down his back in tiny rivulets. He paused when the boys came in. He crooked a finger and wiped the sweat off his brow. The boys greeted him, watched him work for sometime then the twins brought out their football and they played a match.

Kakra always insisted that Panyin be paired with Koku. Though they outnumbered him, he dribbled them and scored. He was fast. Koku had never seen anyone who could run as fast as him.

He was simply magic with the ball. He'd be here one minute and there the next. He couldn't keep up with him. Kakra would be a welcome addition to their football games in school.

Bro. Ebo man threw down his pickaxe and joined the boys in their game. It was now three boys against one man and in no time at all, all three boys were sweating profusely. They were no match for the big burly man. Thirty minutes later, the three boys threw themselves down on the grass and lay panting and gasping for breath. Panyin went in to get a bottle of ice cold water. They drank thirstily.

"What I would really like are some cold mangoes." Kakra said when they had caught their breaths.

"But there are mango trees all over this area, we could go and pluck some."

"You call these..." he stopped and searched for an appropriate word... "these scrawny things you have here mangoes? Kakra asked. "You should have seen what we had in Brong Ahafo. There were mangoes as big as our heads in our backyard and they were sweet and juicy."

"I wonder if anyone has moved into our old house by now." Panyin said whimsically.

"I'm sure the bats are feasting now that we are away." Kakra said.

Bro. Ebo wiped his mouth with the back of his hand and burped loudly. "We have some of those mangoes here as well."

The three boys looked at him in surprise. They had taken long walks in the neighbourhood and had not come across any tree that bore such fruits.

"In the haunted house." He said in answer to their unasked question.

"Is it really haunted?" the boys asked.

"Of course it is; I've heard the ghosts myself."

"Did they talk to you? What did they say? Weren't you scared? What did you go to do there?" They threw the questions at Bro. Ebo, their interest piqued at having met someone who actually had been to the haunted house and had lived to tell his tale.

"What made you go there?" Koku asked.

Bro. Ebo chuckled, "it was *those* same mangoes that your friends described. I was taking a shortcut through the bushes in that area when I saw the tree. No one uses that path anymore. Of course, I'd heard the stories but I just couldn't resist going closer to pluck some of those mangoes. Besides, it was daytime, I didn't think ghosts came out during the day."

"So what happened?"

Bro. Ebo lowered his voice, enjoying himself immensely. It had been a long time since he'd had an audience listen to him with such rapt attention.

He closed his eyes and transported himself to that place and time. "It was a bright sunny day like I said before, the sun was shining and the birds were chirping, I was going along on my way, minding my own business when I caught the smell of the mangoes in the air. It was unlike any other I'd smelled so I literally followed my nose. The tree was right there in front of the house and the branches were literally drooping with fruit. I couldn't resist I grabbed the nearest one and brought it to my lips. It was the most delicious fruit I'd ever tasted. I was still relishing the taste when I HEARD a shout and I SAW the ghost coming out of a window."

"What did it look, like?" Panyin asked enthralled.

"My brother, I didn't hang around to find out. I took off as fast as I could and did not stop running till I got back home."

There was quiet for some time as the children mulled over what they heard.

"But what actually happened in the house. Why is it haunted? Did someone die there?"

Bro. Ebo shrugged. "My grandmother told me that a rich man had the house built for his wife and only child. One night they went out to a party or some other social event, when they came back the house was burning. Trapped inside it were the child and his nanny. The fire gutted half of the house before it was brought under control. The child and nanny were both in the part that had been razed to the ground. The woman rushed into the bushes and wasn't found till three days later. She hung herself. The man moved away afterwards. They say the woman's ghost comes at night looking for the child she lost."

Koku had goose pimples and despite the warm sunlight he shivered.

"Did you ever go back?" Kakra asked thinking of all those ripe mangoes with no one to eat them.

Bro. Ebo started shaking his head before Kakra finished asking the question. "There's absolutely nothing that will make me go back there." He picked his pickaxe and went back to work.

The boys watched him work. Kakra opened his mouth but Panyin spoke first. "Don't even say it. We are not going there."

Kakra turned to Koku, "Imagine getting some of those mango seeds and planting them, then we could have our very own mangoes. Mangoes bigger than our heads."

Panyin turned to protest to Koku against the idiotic proposition his brother had made but he shut his mouth. The gleam in Koku's eye showed he found the idea of growing his own mangoes irresistible. It was two against one. A lost cause. "When do we go?" he asked glumly.

CHAPTER FIFTEEN

A Conversation At Midnight

That night as Kakra dreamed of mangoes as large as his head singing out to him "eat me please, eat me please" and Panyin dreamed of a woman chasing him through a forest crying, "I want my baby, I want my baby," Koku lay awake in his bed thinking.

He wasn't worried about ghosts and he didn't actually want mango seeds. He wanted a healthy branch that he could graft onto some of the mango seedlings in his house. He had never grafted anything before and was excited by the prospect.

He got out of bed and looked for his agric text book. He opened to the chapter on grafting. He dared not turn on the light. His parents would not be happy if they knew he was not asleep. His father, an advocate of regenerative health, believed in having enough sleep.

He found his torchlight and took both the book and the light to his bed and started reading.

Grafting is the act of placing a portion of one plant (bud or scion) into or on a stem, root or branch of another (stock) in such a way that a union will be formed and the partners will continue to grow.

He continued reading about the different methods of grafting, about how to cut, store and protect scions and what the best time for grafting was. The light from the torch began to grow dim. Koku checked the time. It was almost midnight; he'd been reading for almost two hours. He had to sleep now or he'd never wake up on time in the morning for his lessons. He switched off his torch and turned onto his side still excited. He was dozing off when he heard a sound and sat up. He couldn't exactly say what it was but he'd heard it. He got out of bed and tiptoed down the hall. A light glowed dimly from the family room. Was it the TV? His parents forbade them from watching late movies but occasionally he and Sena disobeyed them and snuck downstairs anyway. But if it was the TV how come there was no sound ? He stuck his head round the wall.

Sena was behind the computer her fingers pecking at the keyboard quickly. What was she doing up so late? And who was she chatting with?

He tiptoed closer and stood behind her. She was so caught up in what she was doing she didn't notice he was there. To his dismay, he saw that she was chatting with Big Daddy who still insisted on meeting her. Koku had a bad feeling about this Big Daddy guy. If he wanted to meet his sister why didn't he just come to the house? "Sena" he called out softly. She turned toward him quickly, startled.

"What are you doing here?" she whispered. "Are Mama and Daddy up too?" she wanted to know.

"No, it's just me. I heard something and came to check. What are you doing?"

"Nothing just talking to a friend."

"At this time? Who is he?" Koku asked.

"I already told you, he's just a friend." She avoided looking at him and turned back to the computer screen. She typed some more and shut it down. "Please, don't tell Daddy, she pleaded." She sighed then continued. "He calls himself, 'Big Daddy,' we don't use our real names, she shrugged, we just talk. It's perfectly harmless. He's nice to me. He's 18 and he says I'm beautiful and he loves me." Though the lights were still out there was enough moonlight for Koku to see his sister's eyes glowing. She looked happier than she had been in a really long time. "He wants to meet me she confided."

"Is he coming here then?" Koku asked hopefully.

"No, we'll........" she paused. "No, he's not coming here."

All Koku's doubts came rushing back when he realized what Sena was going to do.

"Don't meet him alone, what if he's not who he says he is?"

"I haven't said I'll meet him, I just said *he* wanted to meet me. And what would be the point of pretending not to be who he says is? We're just chatting. Why would he lie about that?"

Koku did not have an answer to that question but he could not shake off the feeling of the impending doom he felt.

Sena sighed again, "you're a boy, I don't expect you to understand." She was frustrated. Koku wondered what being a boy had to do with anything.

"I know Big Daddy isn't his name but he thinks I'm beautiful. Do you know how that feels?" Koku shook his head. She sighed again, "In school, most boys are friends with me because I'm smart, because they need help with their assignments, even the seniors. But when it is entertainment time no one asks to sit by me or dance with me and now I've found someone who doesn't know I'm smart but still wants to be with me. Do you know what that feels like?"

"But Sena we love you and Daddy is always asking Ami and me to study hard to be like you. Even in school the teachers still say you're the smartest student they ever had. Everyone loves you Sena."

"You're my family; it's your duty to love me. With this boy it feels different, wonderful, that's all." She shrugged. "It makes me feel special. Like the other girls. I just want to meet him this once..... if I don't like him I won't chat with him again. I promise. Please, don't tell Mama or Daddy; please Koku, just this once."

Koku nodded again. Sena smiled and run to her room. Koku went back to his own room. He spent the greater part of the night thinking that he hardly knew his sister. All along, he had thought good grades were all that mattered but apparently there was more to making a person happy than just good grades. Growing up was so complicated he thought as he finally fell asleep.

CHAPTER SIXTEEN

The Haunted House

Mama was very busy the next morning. She had to finish sewing a *slit* and *kaba* for a customer who'd be travelling in two days. Daddy was going to drop Sena off in Tema to visit a friend from school. He would pick her on his way back home from work. It was Koku's duty to babysit Ami. Mama said she did not want to be disturbed.

"But Mama, the twins and I are going exploring today."

"Take her with you." Mama said measuring the cloth and marking it with a piece of chalk. She cut it quickly with her big scissors.

"But Maa....." Koku began then stopped after seeing the look on Mama's face. It was no use grumbling or arguing once Mama had that look on her face.

The twins came promptly at 8am and were not bothered that Ami was to spend the day with them. They thought she was rather cute. Koku did not bother telling them what a nuisance Ami could be. Though he had resolved to be nicer to her they were going to walk a considerable distance and Ami was bound to get tired and demand to be carried back. He went into the kitchen and took a small knife to cut the branches he'd use for the grafts. They set off after promising Mama that they would be back for lunch.

It was a bright sunny day and even Koku could not keep his bad mood. So he joined the twins in laughing at Ami as she chased butterflies. She had given her doll, Yaayaa, to Kakra to hold for her.

After walking for some time they got to the haunted house. In the daylight it looked ordinary enough. The house was old and in ruins. The compound was overgrown with weeds and dried leaves were all over the place. And there right in the middle of the compound was the mango tree. Exactly at the place Bro. Ebo said it would be. But better than anything else, was that, the branches of the tree were laden with the biggest mangoes Koku had ever seen.

"It doesn't look haunted at all." Panyin remarked, a bit disappointed by the dilapidated house.

"What's the meaning of haunted?" Ami asked.

"It means there are ghosts there." Koku told her and laughed when Ami's eyes opened wide in fear. She put her thumb in her mouth and took a step backwards.

"Let's get some mangoes." Kakra said already running to the tree.

"I want to go home." Ami announced.

"We'll get some mangoes then we'll go home. Go and sit on that rock over there," Koku said removing the knife from his pocket.

"I want to go now." Ami said threatening to cry and clutching her doll tighter.

The boys ignored her and the twins started plucking mangoes. Koku climbed the tree to get some choice branches. He was still in the leafy branches when a scream pierced the air. He chuckled and went on with his work. No way were the twins going to scare him. Beneath him the twins looked at each other and back into the tree. "Koku was that you?" Panyin asked. "That's really not funny."

Ami shouted again, "I want to go home now."

They heard the rustling of leaves and Koku's head poked out of the foliage. He looked spooked. "That wasn't me." He was still looking at them when they heard the scream again. It sounded like a banshee wailing. He was so frightened he lost his grip on the branch he was holding and fell out of the tree.

The boys looked at each other. The mangoes were quickly forgotten as Koku jumped to his feet, grabbed Ami and they took to their heels. Another scream sounded and they heard movement in the old house. It sounded like someone was trying to open a door. The boys did not turn to find out who it was. Along the way Koku tripped and lost his grip on Ami. She fell and scraped her knee which started to bleed. Panyin carried her and they run all the way to Koku's house. They collapsed on the veranda panting. Ami was in tears and she wouldn't stop howling.

Mama came out to find out what all the commotion was about. She cleaned Ami's cut and took her inside but Ami wouldn't stop crying especially when she realized Yaayaa had been left behind at the haunted house.

"The ghost will eat her, the ghost will eat her," she sobbed.

"What's all this about ghosts?" Mama asked. She was very angry. Koku narrated the whole story.

"There must be some reasonable explanation for all this," Mama said. "We'll wait for your father to come home; he'll go and bring the doll."

CHAPTER SEVENTEEN

Rescuers?

It was Mawuga's turn to act as a look out. He didn't expect today to be any different. He took his seat by the ventilation hole and stared outside. Nothing had changed. He could describe this scene in his sleep. No one ever came here. The night they'd brought him it had been very dark. He hadn't been able to see anything and ever since then all he ever saw was this mango tree with fruits they couldn't get to.

The other children were playing a game of ludo. Kwame Joe as usual was cheating and the others were keeping a close eye on him. Adoley had sliced a loaf of bread and was spreading margarine on the slices. He took another look outside. Nothing had changed; not that he expected it to but it would be so good to get out of this place. The first and only time Kwame Joe had asked Jagger why he was keeping them the big man had pounced on him and nearly beaten him to a pulp. Nancy had looked on unconcerned. He and Adoley had tried to pull him off the poor boy but Jagger had flung them away with such force that they had landed at the other end of the room. With his face still contorted with fury he had turned to the rest of them and asked if they had any more questions. The younger children had slunk away to their beds in fear. No one had dared ask another question since then.

He got lost in his thoughts again. He didn't particularly miss his home. He came from a fishing village near the sea. His father had been a rich fisherman and had had four wives. Life had been bearable till the sea had begun eating their land. As the sea inched closer and closer inland his father had sunk deeper and deeper into despair. His land, land he'd inherited from his father and that had been in his family for many generations was gone. Of his five canoes, only one was sea worthy and the income from that canoe was not enough to cater for his four wives and their twelve children. One day his father had taken the canoe out to sea and never returned. A search party had been sent to look out for him. All that was found was the empty canoe adrift on the high seas.

He and his siblings were distributed to the rest of his father's relatives. The night before he was to leave he stole some money and left for Accra. He found work at the outskirts of the town in a stone quarry. It was backbreaking work. He was up at 5am each morning and at his designated spot with a pile of rocks half his height. He had a sledge hammer which he used to break the rocks. He worked from dawn to dusk each day breaking the rocks into smaller pieces. At the end of the day he was paid GH1. He slept in a wooden shed with other children his age. He had run away when one child had fallen into a quarry and died. Work had gone on as usual; the owners of the quarry had not put up any barricades or done anything else to prevent further accidents.

He had met Jagger shortly afterwards who had promised to find him a better job. He brought him to this room in this house where he met the other children. The food here was much better than all he had had in his entire life but what was mind boggling was the uncertainty. How long would they be kept here in this room? And afterwards where would they be sent? Why were they being fattened up?

He peeped outside. A movement caught his eye. He looked and did not believe what he was seeing. He rubbed his eyes and looked again. Three children were outside. Two boys were plucking mangoes and a little girl sat on a rock a little distance away from them sucking her thumb. He was so surprised he stood for a full minute without moving. Then he turned to the other children, "there are people here," he screamed to the others. He put his mouth to the ventilation hole and shouted. The other children rushed to his hole. They took turns in looking outside. It was the only one that offered a good view of the boys. There was a full minute of silence before reality set in and they started shouting but the children outside seemed to be frozen into place.

"It's not working," Adoley said in frustration, "I'm sure they can hear us but why are they just standing there. We have to try something else."

"Let's bang the walls with something, they all rushed back to look for tools, anything they could use to make some noise." Kwame Joe tossed the mattress off the nearest bed and picked up a plank of wood. The bigger children followed his example, the smaller children armed themselves with spoons and shoes and they made as much of a racket as they could. Mawuga was looking out the peep hole.

"They've heard us!" he cried happily, "a third boy has jumped out of the tree."

"We're going to be rescued," Faustie squealed in delight.

Mawuga turned to look at the others. They were all so excited. To think that in just a few minutes, they'd be out of this place. They'd be free. Kwame Joe dropped his plank, jostled him out of the way and looked through the hole. He couldn't believe what he was seeing.

"No, wait" he tried calling out to the children. "Don't go, wait!" He rushed for his plank and began hitting the wall again. Mawuga turned to look through the hole. He couldn't believe it the children were running as though they were being chased by a dozen dogs with rabies.

He dropped to the floor, buried his head in his hands and wept. The other children again took turns in looking out. The children were gone. The young children joined Mawuga on the floor in crying. Adoley and Kwame Joe didn't know what to do as well. They couldn't believe they had come this close to being rescued and had blown it.

CHAPTER EIGHTEEN

Big Daddy

Meanwhile in Tema, Sena had met Helen, her classmate from school. She made Helen swear to keep a secret then she told her all about Big Daddy and how they had both agreed to meet later that afternoon.

Now, Helen absolutely adored Sena. She thought she was extremely smart. While Helen spent hours studying her notes, Sena only had to read through once or twice to remember everything. Helen was the sort of girl who was a good follower. She never disagreed with what anyone said because she wanted them to like her so when Sena told her about her meeting with Big Daddy, she paid no attention to her misgivings and promised to keep Sena's secret. "I'll be back at your house by 4pm. My father will come for me at 6pm." Sena told her, she was so happy she couldn't keep still. "You're such a good friend." She gushed. Helen smiled, glad that someone as smart as Sena thought so highly of her.

Sena left Helen's house feeling on top of the world. She'd carefully chosen her outfit. Skinny black jeans, a white blouse and a wide black belt. She dabbed some lip gloss onto her lips and brushed her short cropped hair backwards. Her mother would not let her use make-up but the lip gloss was better than nothing.

She got to the fast food joint thirty minutes early. She ordered a coke but was too nervous to drink. She straightened her clothes and thought belatedly that she shouldn't have worn a white blouse. She hoped she did not look like a chorister or a waitress. She wanted to look hot. She spent the time studying people as they walked through the door wondering which one would approach her and turn out to be Big Daddy.

No, not that one she hoped. He looked dirty with his baggy shorts and dirty boxers.

Not that one either he was nice but he looked younger than 18. She was so engrossed in her assessment that she didn't notice when a grown man slid into the booth next to her.

"Sorry, that seat is taken, I'm waiting for someone." She checked her watch. Big Daddy was late. It was ten minutes past noon.

"Hi, Anes," the man said smiling. Sena nearly choked on her drink. The man must have been about 45. He was obscenely fat, nothing like the muscular eighteen year old she'd been expecting. He was already going bald. The neck and armpits of his t-shirt were soaked with sweat."

He offered his hand and smiled again, "I'm big Daddy."

"You said you were eighteen!" She accused.

"I lied." He said simply, "besides I told you were too young for me and *you* said age was nothing but a number."

He was right Sena realized. At the time, she'd thought she was being sexy and coy, now she realized she'd been foolish to agree to meet him.

"Relax," Big Daddy said noticing her growing discomfort. "Have I treated you wrong before?"

She shook her head. "No."

"Have I insulted you before?"

"No."

"Haven't I always supported you when your parents misunderstood you?"

"Yes."

"Have I asked you to do anything you didn't want to?"

"No."

"Don't I treat you like the adult you are? Sixteen is an adult you know?"

"Yes."

"Do you think I'm capable of hurting you?"

She hesitated.

"Sena, answer me." Big Daddy said.

"How do you know my name?" She asked.

The man grinned revealing discoloured teeth. "Anes, Sena, there wasn't much to figure out."

For the first time Sena felt truly frightened.

"Let's go somewhere quieter and talk." He suggested.

"I like it here," Sena said.

"I thought you said you wanted to be treated like an adult, this place is for kids, it's cheap, there's another restaurant near here, it's quieter, classier and their food is good too. Come on, Sena, let's go."

Big Daddy led the way and she followed him outside to his car. He asked her to fasten her seat belt which she did. They were still in the parking lot of the fast food joint when hands reached out from behind the seat and a handkerchief was used to cover her nose. She tried to fight but the seat belt held her down and in a matter of seconds she passed out.

CHAPTER NINETEEN

Kidnapped

When Sena came to, she was lying on a bed, bound and gagged in a dark room. She tried to wriggle her hands out of her restraints but failed. The ropes just cut deeper and deeper into her flesh. She was hungry and thirsty but too terrified to register these fundamental human needs. She didn't know how long she'd been unconscious and didn't know what time it was. The curtains were drawn across the windows and she couldn't tell if it was night or still day time.

She heard muffled voices coming closer. A key turned in the lock. A shaft of light from the corridor illuminated a corner of the room. Then she made out the silhouette of a man. He was as thin as a stick. He looked sick. His clothes just hang on him like they were too big for him. He kept tugging his trousers up. He must have been the second man in the car who gagged her. He stood watching her for a long time. Then he shut the door and left.

After what seemed to be a long time, Big Daddy himself entered the room. He switched on the light and marched straight to the bed. The bed creaked under his weight as he sat.

"You told me, you've never had a boyfriend before, is that true?" He looked very worried.

Sena nodded.

"So you must be a virgin, right?"

Sena didn't like where this was going but she nodded. What did her virginity have to do with anything?

Big Daddy sighed with relief. Then he turned towards her. "You have to help my son, please" He begged. Tears came to his eyes and he wiped them with the back of his hand. "You are our only hope, please." He pulled out a dirty handkerchief and blew his nose noisily.

Sena was bewildered. What did she have that this man and his son wanted? She was only sixteen years. How much money did they think she had?

"You have to help us. My son has AIDS. He was HIV positive for three years and we didn't know. He got diarrhoea which wouldn't go away and the doctors tested him. He's only nineteen. We've done everything. Tried everything. Gone from hospital to hospital, herbalist to herbalist, prayer camp to prayer camp. He's a good boy, a little unruly but that's how boys are, I don't want him to die....... See how skinny he is. Every two weeks he falls sick, if it's not malaria, it's an infection. Please help him, he's too young to die, I don't want him to die, please don't let him die....... he's my only child, please help him."

Help you do what? Sena wondered. As if Big Daddy could read her mind he said, "Someone told me if he has sex with a virgin, he'll be healed."

Sena was mortified. This man was crazy. Absolutely crazy. His son was going to infect her with HIV. How could he believe that *that* would make his son better? She started sobbing. She wished she'd never met this man, never gone to that chat room on the internet, never agreed to follow him to his car. She just wanted to go home.

"Will you help us?" he asked, his voice had grown colder. He began clenching his fingers. The vein in his neck stood out and his nostrils flared. Sena noticed the change in his demeanour. She lay still. He slapped her hard and his hand clamped down on her throat. She screamed into the gag, he was strangling her. He started screaming. "I asked you a question, you silly girl, answer me! Answer me! Will you help us?" The younger man rushed into the room and tried to pull Big Daddy off Sena.

"Stop it, you'll kill her! Stop it!" The boy begged.

Big Daddy let go, he turned to his son. "Can't you see I'm doing this for you? Can't you see?"

He began pacing up and down in the room, looking from Sena to his son. "I'm going out, do *it* before I come back." Big Daddy stormed out of the room.

The young man turned to Sena. "I'm going to take out the gag. If you scream my father will kill you for sure, understand?" Sena nodded. The man drew neared. Now that the lights were out she saw how young he was. He was thin, much thinner than she'd realized and very sick. Even talking was an effort she realized. He was breathing heavily through his mouth. She squirmed when he touched her. His skin was as hot as an iron. He removed the gag. She drew in ragged breaths. The boy sat by her on the bed. "I'm sorry he hurt you." He said and stroked her face. She moved her head away. He pulled her shirt up and unbuttoned her jeans.

"This wouldn't make you better you know? Sena said to him. "You should be in a hospital and take medicine. The drugs are free. They told us so in school. I can't make you better. You have to believe me." He stopped undressing her. Sena continued talking realizing that the only way she was going to get out of this place was if the boy helped her. "I'm sorry, you're sick, really I am, but I can't heal you.... I'm only sixteen, you'll infect me with the virus if you do what your father wants, please...." he lay watching her for sometime then dropped down on the bed by her side.

"What's your name?" he asked after a long silence.

"Sena." Sena's heart beat fast. What should she do now? What if his father came back? What if the boy changed his mind? She had to get out of this place fast.

"Sena" he repeated, "it's a beautiful name, what does it mean?"

"God's gift."

He lapsed into silence for some time then said "I wish God would give me a gift of health."

"How old are you?"

"Sixteen"

"How did you meet my Dad?"

"In a chat room on the internet."

He started crying softly. "I don't want to die. I'm only nineteen. You're the third girl my father has brought me. The others didn't work."

Sena gulped. He'd already infected two other girls! The boy continued crying by her side. She started crying as well. "Please, let me go, I beg you, let me go before your Father comes, please."

CHAPTER TWENTY

Sena Cannot Be Found

Helen stood crying in front of Mr. Amegatsey and her parents. She was not worried at all when Sena wasn't back at 4pm like she promised. She was probably having so much fun with her new friend. But when the clock struck 5pm and she was still not backHelen began to worry. She did know what to do. At 5: 30pm she told her mother what had happened. Her mother, Mrs. Amamoo, had called Sena's father who had come over right away.

They went to the fast food restaurant and asked if anyone had seen her. One waiter remembered seeing her by the window with a fat man but he wasn't much help. He couldn't tell where they'd gone. He couldn't even describe the man except that he was fat and was sweating very much which the waiter had thought was strange considering that it wasn't hot outside and the room was air conditioned.

Mr. Amegatsey had gone to the police station to file a missing person's report. The policeman on duty told him a person could only be declared as missing if he had disappeared for more than twenty-fours. So Mr. Amegatsey had tried to file a kidnapping report. The policeman said from Mr. Amegatsey's narration, it appeared Sena had not been coerced to go with the fat man. She had gone willingly. He tried giving Mr. Amegatsey some advice. "Teenagers do these things all the time, just go home and relax; she'll come when she's ready."

Mr. Amegatsey asked, "Do you have children?"

The man looked surprised. "No."

"When you have your children and they go off with a stranger see if you can go home and relax."

Mr. Amegatsey and the Amamoos drove to all the eateries in the vicinity but Sena wasn't found. They drove through all the streets searching. They even checked the emergency rooms of two clinics in case she'd been in an accident but there was no trace of Sena.

Helen was still crying. "It's not your fault," Mr. Amegatsey told her, "maybe she's already gone home or asleep somewhere." He tried comforting her but his words sounded hollow in his own ears. There was nothing to do but to go home. After obtaining a promise from the Amamoos to call if they heard anything about Sena's whereabouts, he drove home.

When he got home he called his wife into their bedroom and broke the news to her. She let out a loud wail and threw herself onto the floor, her hands clasped over her head.

"I'm dead O, I'm dead O!" she cried.

Koku and Ami rushed to their parents' bedroom. Mr. Amegatsey told them what had happened. Ami started crying and joined her mother on the floor. Koku didn't know what to say. He felt ridden with guilt. If he'd told his parents about Big Daddy maybe Sena would be home now. Mr. Amegatsey sat on the floor beside his wife and daughter and pulled them both to him. He tried to console them but they were inconsolable. He held them as they cried. Later when his wife had calmed down sufficiently he tucked her into bed. She was still sobbing and saying "O Sena, O Sena" but she fell asleep shortly afterwards. Mr. Amegatsey had carried Ami who had also fallen asleep to the girls' room but he hadn't been able to put her down in her own bed when he saw Sena's empty bed. He carried her back to his room and put her beside her mother.

He found Koku sitting in the dark in the living room. The TV set was on. The parents of the girl who had been kidnapped were on the screen. They were offering a GH 10,000 reward for anyone who had information on their daughter. Mr. Amegatsey sat by Koku and hugged the boy to himself. To Koku's surprise his father started crying.

"I thought men are not supposed to cry." Koku said.

His father held him tighter and said "sometimes it takes a real man to cry."

Koku hugged his father and told him everything. Then he started crying himself. "It's my fault, she's gone, it's my fault."

His father wiped his tears away with his thumb. "No, it's not."

"But it is," he insisted, "sometimes I've wished that something would happen to her so that you wouldn't always compare me to her, so that you'd be proud of me and now this has happened and I just want her to come back. I want her to come back," he cried.

Mr. Amegatsey was silent for a long while. He had not known his son felt this way. He had not even had an inkling. He wished he could go back into time and change everything. He held his only son close to him. There was still so much he had to learn about being a father he realized.

"Dear God please let me find my daughter," he prayed.

CHAPTER TWENTY ONE

A Miraculous Escape

At 1 in the morning the phone in the Amegatsey house rang interrupting the fitful sleep of Mr. Amegatsey. It was Mr. Amamoo, Helen's father. Sena had come to their house. Mr. Amegatsey quickly woke up his wife. They bundled the still sleeping Ami and Koku into the car and drove to the Amamoos. A badly shaken but very much alive Sena was wrapped in a blanket sitting by Mrs. Amamoo and Helen. Her hands were shaking so much she kept spilling the mug of Milo drink Mrs. Amamoo had given her.

Mrs. Amegatsey carried her daughter and set her on her own lap. Cradling her and rocking her. Tears flowed freely all around. Ami was the only one still asleep. When Sena had calmed down sufficiently she told them everything that had happened. She left nothing out. Her mother just kept crying.

"He let me go." Sena said still crying. "He said he knew he was dying and then he cut off the ropes, gave me my bag and he let me out of the house. I was so afraid I'd meet his father but I didn't. I ran out of the house till I got to a street, then I asked a taxi driver to bring me here, I'm so sorry" she cried. "Thank you God, thank you God." Mr. Amegatsey said as he hugged his daughter.

The Amegatseys thanked the Amamoos and took their daughter back home with them. That night the entire family slept in the master bedroom. Mrs. Amegatsey wanted all her children around her. In the early hours of the morning they fell asleep.

The next morning Mr. and Mrs. Amegatsey took Sena to the police station. The policemen got her to describe Big Daddy and she did. But she didn't know his name or his son's name. She couldn't even remember the directions to his house. The policemen shook their heads sadly at Mr. Amegatsey and said "there's nothing else we can do."

"But you heard her story," Mr. Amegatsey fumed. "This man could lure more innocent girls for his son to defile and infect with the virus. He has already done it twice!"

"We don't have a name, no car number, she doesn't even know the area to which she was taken and he never sent her a picture of himself. We can't even track him using the internet; he'll just stop using the name Big Daddy and use something else. He'll go to another chat room or social networking site. These men are predators. They know how not to leave a trail. We are aware they are out there but there is very little we can do stop. It's mainly up to you the parents to monitor which sites your children are on."

There was nothing to do but to leave. Life gradually settled down to normal after that. Mr. Amegatsey made appointments with the PTA board in his children's school to talk to parents and teachers about what his daughter had gone through. Mrs. Amegatsey talked to the mothers in the Women's Fellowship at her church. Sena herself talked to friends she knew who used internet chat rooms. Mr. Amegatsey took the time to listen to his children, to what they wanted to be, to their interests. He was surprised at what he found out. Sena felt pressurized to give off her best academically. She felt the only reason her father loved her was because she was a good student. Though she was a science student she didn't want medicine as her profession. She wanted to be a journalist.

Then it was Koku's turn to speak. Koku didn't want to be a medic either. He wanted to be a farmer. He wanted to study agricultural science in secondary school. Even when he didn't get aggregate 6 he wanted his father to be proud that he had done better in some subjects than the term before. That afternoon he took his entire family up to see his secret garden. His mother was impressed by the size of the ripening tomatoes and pepper. His father was astounded at his son's capabilities.

Ami said she wanted to be a dancer. Mr. Amegatsey said that was ok. Then she changed her mind and said she wanted to be a nurse. He said that was ok too. Then she said she wanted to be a nurse and a dancer. He picked her up twirled her in the air and said she could be anything she wanted to be.

The day Sena's school reopened Mr. Amegatsey drove her to school. Koku accompanied them. "Everything we do or leave undone in this world has a repercussion." He told them. "Sometimes bad things happen as a result of certain decisions or choices we make, Sena, you knew we wouldn't approve of what you were doing but you did it anyway. What happened to you is a result of a choice you made. Wanting to be treated as an adult does not just mean you are free to do as you like, you must know that it comes with responsibilities to yourself and to others. You were lucky to get away unharmed and we thank God for your life but there are so many others who might not be so lucky. Being an adult doesn't mean you don't ask for advice or for help. Actually, a mature adult is one who isn't afraid to take his time to think things through properly before doing them or to ask for help if he feels a little confused or overwhelmed. If you can't come to me or your mother, you have your teachers in school and your Sunday school teachers and pastors in church. There are a whole lot of people to share your problems with, no matter what they are."

He paused "and Sena if your mother and I haven't told you before, I'm saying it now, we'd love you whether or not you were brainy. You're a beautiful young woman and we know someday you'll meet a nice young man who will treat you well." He paused and looked at his two teenage children realizing what an awkward phase of life they were in. They were not exactly adults and yet they were not exactly children either.

"Your mother and I discussed this, you can come home yourself over the midterms," he said to Sena when they got to her dormitory.

Sena hugged her Father tight. "I want you to come for me Daddy. I have two years left to be a child and I want to enjoy each second of those two years."

Mr. Amegatsey smiled and wiped a stray tear from his face.

CHAPTER TWENTY TWO

The Haunted House Again

Now that Koku had his Father's permission to pursue a carrier in crop science, he desperately wanted to graft a branch from the mango tree in front of the haunted house to his mango seedlings. He had to go back. He broached the subject to the twins, they both said a vehement No! There was no way they were going back there! Then Kakra changed his mind and agreed to go with Koku. Panyin on the other hand wasn't so easy to convince.

"I thought you'd help me find Ami's doll, she still cries at night for it." Koku said trying his best to look crestfallen.

"Sure, this is all about Yaayaa," Panyin said sarcastically, "it has nothing to with you wanting those branches for your graft and you," he pointed to Kakra "fantasizing about cold sliced mangoes and pawpaw with a dash of lemon juice." Kakra had seen the dessert on a cooking programme on TV the day before.

Then Panyin shook his head, "I'm only going because of Yaayaa." Koku and Kakra whooped with joy.

"Was it really a ghost?" Panyin asked.

The other boys shrugged. None of them wanted to think about what had happened the last time they went there.

"Let's get going." Koku cried itching to get started. "Ghost or no ghost, I'm going to get those grafts."

"Ghosts or no ghosts, I'm going to get those mangoes." Kakra said to which Panyin sighed dolefully.

"Mama said the Meteorological Service said there would a be storm this afternoon. She wants me to home before it starts." Koku told the twins as he went home for his knife.

Kakra got a basket and they set off. Panyin kept muttering that it was a bad idea but he followed them anyway. The closer they got to the haunted house, the quieter they got. "Do what you have to do quickly so we can leave this place, it's very creepy." Panyin said noticing Yaayaa on the rock Ami had been sitting on and going to pick her. The pile of mangoes they'd gathered the last time had began to rot. Koku was soon in the branches of the thick leafy tree. He was as agile as a monkey. Kakra began plucking the mangoes.

Out of nowhere, two people jumped out of the bushes and caught the twins. "We knew you'd come back, you pesky kids, tell us what do you know?"

Panyin and Kakra both screamed. The ghosts had come for them and the ghosts could talk.

"What do you know?" the man asked.

"What do we know about what?" Panyin asked trembling.

The man who held Panyin had a huge scar running from the corner of his left eye to the corner of his mouth. His nose was flat and he wore dark sunglasses. It was Jagger but neither Panyin nor Kakra knew that.

It had begun to drizzle and in the distance they could hear peals of thunder.

"Are you the only ones here?" the woman who'd grabbed Kakra asked. Vaguely he wondered if she was the woman who'd lost her son in the fire. He was not going to let her use him to replace his lost child. He looked down at her feet. She was wearing sandals. He raised his foot and brought it down hard on her foot.

"They're not ghosts, Panyin," Kakra called out to his brother who was still trembling. The woman yelled but did not loosen his grip on him. Instead she slapped him twice in rapid succession.

"Let us go we haven't done anything wrong." Panyin pleaded.

"Answer the question! Are you the only ones here?"

"Well, do you see anyone apart from us?" Kakra asked his cheek still burning from the slap. The woman raised her leg and hit him. He was caught off guard and fell on the ground. He hit his head on a piece a rock and sunk into unconsciousness. The rain was coming down faster.

"It's just us!" Panyin shouted. He was very frightened of these people. "No one knows we are here, we came for the mangoes." Jagger and Nancy did not look convinced.

"How about the doll? You're both boys, too old to play with dolls, who is the doll for?"

"It's for our little sister, we came here with her and she left it behind."

"What did you come here for?" Jagger asked.

"We came here for mangoes." Panyin pointed at the pile of rotting mangoes.

"So why didn't you take them." Nancy wanted to know.

"We heard a noise and were scared. We thought the ghosts were coming for us."

"You thought there were ghosts yet you came back today. Why?" Nancy wanted to know.

"Our little sister has been crying for the doll so we had to come back and we decided to get some mangoes as well. Please let us go, we'll never ever come back here," he pleaded.

"I believe them but we can't let them go, let's put them with the other children." Jagger said.

"Are you crazy? Didn't you hear what he said? His little sister knows this place. If these two boys don't go back home, their parents will come here and find them and the other children. We have to leave now." Nancy was fuming.

"We can't move them, not without the truck. We'll wait for the rain to stop, and then we'll bring the truck, take the other children and find a new place." Jagger said.

"We can't wait for the rain to stop, we'll leave now. This place is no longer safe, besides the police are still looking for that other girl, I told you it was a bad idea to take her but no, you didn't listen, you never listen." Nancy snapped and snatched Panyin away from Jagger. The rain had plastered her hair down her face but she still looked pretty. Vaguely Panyin wondered how someone who was this beautiful could be so callous. She led him into the haunted house. Jagger hefted Kakra onto his shoulders and followed them into the haunted house.

A few minutes later, they both came out still arguing and disappeared into the bushes.

CHAPTER TWENTY THREE

Koku Gets Help

The rain was coming down in torrents. Koku saw the man and woman come out of the house. Faintly he heard the sound of an engine starting. He couldn't be sure if the vehicle was really gone. He counted to three hundred at what he thought were one minute intervals before he jumped down.

He had parted the branches and seen and heard everything that had happened. His respect for the twins went up another notch. They had been very brave to say they were the only ones there. He crept into the haunted house, thankful for the occasional bolts of lightning that lighted his way.

"Kakra! Panyin!" he called out but the rain drowned out his voice. Water dripped from holes in the roof and flooded the floor. He waded through the water, going from room to room till he stopped. This was odd, he thought. Everything in this ramshackle house was falling apart but here was a sturdy mahogany door.

He rammed it as hard as he could and called out, "Panyin! Kakra!"

"Koku is that you?" Panyin called back. "There are seven children here; the missing girl we saw on TV is here too."

"Yes, it's me; I'll try to open the door." Koku cried with relief trying to force the door open but it wouldn't budge. He removed his knife and tried to slide it into the lock but the door still wouldn't budge.

Suddenly a cacophony of voices called out.

"Just leave the door and get help before they come back."

"Quick, get some help. Get the police."

"Save us please"

Then he heard Panyin's voice. "Koku, Kakra has been injured; he's bleeding from a wound in his head. We have to get him to a hospital quickly."

Koku didn't wait to be told a second time. He ran through the rain, slipping and falling down in the mud a number of times till he got to the police station.

CHAPTER TWENTY FOUR

Free At Last!

The first policeman Koku saw listened in silence as he narrated his story not sure whether or not to believe that the young girl the police had been searching for was right here in their own backyard. Then he left him and got his chief. The man looked at the young boy. He was soaked to the skin, dripping wet from the rain and making a fine puddle on his linoleum floor. If what the boy was saying was true then they had to act quickly to get the kidnappers.

He got his men together and they went over a simple plan to get the kidnappers. "Sergeant, get this young man some warm clothes, a blanket and a cup of warm Milo."

"Please sir, let me go with you." Koku begged.

The man looked at him, "there might be gunfire if the kidnappers resist, and I don't want you in the way."

Koku looked crestfallen. "But," the Chief continued, "If you promise to be quiet and to stay with one of my men, you can come." He ordered someone to telephone Auntie Aggie and Mrs. Amegatsey and they left.

Koku sat beside the chief in the backseat of one of the patrol cars. He had begun to shiver in his wet clothes. The chief put a blanket around him and went back to issuing instructions on his walkie- talkie. The chief looked very smart in his blue uniform and shining black shoes. Koku couldn't help smiling to himself. Just wait till he told Manuel and the boys in school that he'd ridden in a police car. A few metres from the haunted house, the police hid their cars in a thicket and divided themselves into three groups. One group stalked the area; the second went into the house and got all the children out. They were whisked away to safety in two police cars with sirens. The third group waited in the room for the kidnappers.

Kakra was taken to a hospital. The doctor said he'd had a concussion and would be fine but he still wanted to keep him for a day or two for observation.

The kidnappers were arrested. They broke down during the interrogation and confessed that they ran a child trafficking syndicate. They kidnapped children and smuggled them out of the country. Some were sold as sex slaves to paedophiles and brothel owners; others were used as cheap labour on plantations and in factories. They had been using the haunted house as a hide-out for a number of years. They realized that the myth kept away curious people and any unusual sound or activity there had been attributed to ghosts. They named all the other members of the syndicate and the police arrested them as well.

All the captured children were reunited with their families. Malik was still not talking. The doctors said he'd been traumatised by the abduction but he was making slow progress. Naa Teiki's parents put Kwame Joe, Adoley, Mawuga and Faustie back into school and promised to pay for their upkeep. The GH ¢10,000 reward had been given to the three boys as promised. Their parents put the money into education funds for them.

CHAPTER TWENTY FIVE

All's Well That Ends Well

K akra was discharged and went back home. He had developed an appetite in the hospital and was making up for lost time. The boys were sitting on the veranda enjoying an afternoon breeze while they ate their lunch. Auntie Aggie had outdone herself. They were eating big balls of *fufu* and light soup with chicken. Kakra cracked a bone with and sucked out the marrow. They talked of nothing but the adventure they had had at the haunted house all afternoon. "Mr. Ankamah was right" Koku said thoughtfully, "slavery still exists in this country."

"To think the house wasn't really haunted after all!" said Panyin licking his fingers noisily.

Koku was about to put a piece of chicken into his mouth when Kakra said "do you know what would make a very nice dessert after this meal?"

Koku shook his head and chewed his chicken.

Panyin groaned aloud. "Don't even say it, we're not going back."

Kakra said it anyway, "sliced cold mangoes and pawpaw with a dash of lemon juice."

"I agree totally," Koku said thinking of his grafts "and I know just the place to get those mangoes."

Panyin picked up his empty bowl. "You two are indefatigable." He said trying out a word he'd learnt recently.

"But Panyin," Koku said mischievously, "Yaayaa is still up there and Ami would be happy to get her back."

"For Ami! The only reason I'll go back there is for Ami."

Koku smiled, happy and satisfied that he had such good friends.